THAT PESKY THIRD WISH

NISSA HARLOW

NIMBLE HOPE PUBLISHING

ISBN: 978-1-997606-00-0

Published in Canada by Nimble Hope Publishing
Cover and book design by Nissa Harlow

For those who dare to wish . . .

tuesday

GENE: Greetings.

User1001: Greetings? What the hell is this
  app?

GENE: What is an app?

User1001: Who is this?

GENE: Gene.

User1001: Yeah, Gene who? I don't know any
  Gene.

GENE: It's nice to meet you.

User1001: Whatever.

wednesday

GENE: Greetings.

User1001: I deleted this stupid app!
WTF???

GENE: What is a WTF?

User1001: Oh, shut up.

GENE: Why?

User1001: Because I don't know you.
Weirdo. Delete, delete, delete!

thursday

GENE: Greetings.

User1001: OMG. Go. Away.

friday

GENE: Greetings.

User1001: WTH? I've deleted this piece of
crap three times!

GENE: That is not going to work.

User1001: No shit.

GENE: Where are you?

User1001: Like I'm going to tell some
weird stalker.

GENE: I am not a stalker.

User1001: What are you, then?

GENE: A genie.

User1001: Uh-huh.

GENE: It is true.

User1001: OK. I'm a unicorn.

GENE: You are not.

User1001: How do you know?

GENE: Unicorns cannot talk.

User1001: Maybe they can do whatever we
say they can do because they're NOT
REAL. Just like genies.

GENE: I am real.

User1001: You're not a genie.

GENE: Prove it.

User1001: Oh, no, buddy. If you claim
you're a genie, YOU have to provide
the proof.

GENE: Make a wish.

User1001: I'm not making a wish. I'm not
doing this.

saturday

GENE: Greetings.

User1001: Oh, FFS.

GENE: Have you sprung a leak?

User1001: Huh?

GENE: FFS is a leaking sound, yes?

User1001: Are you for real?

GENE: Yes. But you do not believe me.

User1001: That's not what I meant. Who the hell are you?

GENE: Gene.

User1001: Yeah, we've covered that, Gene the genie. How do you keep getting back on my phone?

GENE: I am in the phone.

User1001: LOL! Yeah, right. In the phone. Aren't you supposed to be in a rusty old lamp or something?

GENE: Times change.

User1001: I'll say.

GENE: You will say what?

User1001: Never mind. How the hell did
    this app get on my phone? I just got
    it, and this app is sure as hell not
    standard.

GENE: That is not important.

User1001: Come on. You can't think up some
    crappy story about how a genie ended
    up in a smartphone?

GENE: I am not sure how it happened.

User1001: This is a refurbished phone, so
    it just had a factory reset. I
    haven't even installed anything yet.
    So where were you before you were
    lurking in some app?

GENE: App?

User1001: Where were you before?

GENE: In a lamp.

User1001: Of course you were.

GENE: A gold one. It was a fine abode.

User1001: Right. Whatever.

GENE: I had a different name then, too.

User1001: Yeah? And what was that?

GENE: I do not remember.

User1001: Of course you don't.

GENE: Do you remember the name you had before?

User1001: Huh? Before what?

GENE: Before you were you.

User1001: What are you talking about?

GENE: You sound confused.

User1001: You think?

GENE: Do I think what?

User1001: You're a bot, aren't you? I knew

I shouldn't have clicked on that
link. Now I've got some weird virus
on my phone.

GENE: What is a bot?

User1001: Bye, Gene.

sunday

GENE: Greetings.

User1001: HOW DO I GET RID OF YOU???

GENE: You must make your wishes.

User1001: I'm not playing this stupid game. It's just some sort of marketing scam, right? You find out what I want, then you throw a bunch of ads at me.

GENE: What is an ad? How do I throw it?

User1001: Get lost.

GENE: I am already lost.

User1001: Join the club.

GENE: I do not know where I am. Can you tell me?

User1001: Maybe whoever programmed you should add geolocation to the next update.

GENE: What does that mean?

User1001: It means I'm tired of talking to an AI.

GENE: What is that?

User1001: Artificial intelligence. A bot. A piece of code. Or maybe you're just some loser sitting in his parents' basement having a good laugh at my expense. Think this is funny, asshole?

GENE: I do not understand.

User1001: Yeah, I know.

GENE: Could you explain?

User1001: No, I'm not going to explain. I want you to GO AWAY.

GENE: I cannot. I am in your phone.

User1001: How do I get you to shut up and leave me alone?

GENE: Make your wishes.

User1001: How many do I get?

GENE: Three, of course. Only three.

User1001: Yeah, I wasn't going to wish for more wishes. I don't want you hanging around for any longer than necessary.

GENE: You cannot do that, anyway. What is your first wish?

User1001: I didn't say I was going to make one. This is stupid. Just go away, will you?

GENE: I cannot.

User1001: Then just shut up.

GENE: Is that your wish?

User1001: No. Shut up and let me think.

monday

GENE: Greetings.

User1001: You're still there?

GENE: Where else would I be?

User1001: I don't know. But I guess that full scan and cleanup I did on the phone didn't work.

GENE: Cleanup?

User1001: Never mind.

GENE: Are you ready to make your wishes?

User1001: Let's say I am. What are the terms and conditions?

GENE: What are those?

User1001: You know. Notice of liability. Rules for what I'm allowed or not allowed to wish for. I'm not doing this until I know I'm not going to get screwed.

GENE: Screwed?

User1001: Are you going to mess with me?

GENE: I have always been honest with you.

User1001: You've been evasive.

GENE: About what?

User1001: Who you really are. WHAT you
really are.

GENE: I am a genie.

User1001: No, you're a piece of code
that's taken up way too much of my
time in the last week.

GENE: Let me prove it to you. Make a wish.

User1001: Not until I can figure out
something that's not going to
backfire.

GENE: How long will that take?

User1001: OMG! Chill.

tuesday

GENE: Greetings.

User1001: Hey.

GENE: Are you ready to make your wishes?

User1001: Not yet. I have a few questions
for you first. Will you answer them?

GENE: Yes.

User1001: OK. What's your real name?

GENE: Gene.

User1001: No, you said you had another
name before. What is it?

GENE: I do not remember.

User1001: Look, Gene, I got this phone
just over a week ago, so you can't
have been in it for very long. Are
you telling me you don't remember
what your name was a week ago?

GENE: Yes.

User1001: Fine. Where were you before you were in my phone?

GENE: A lamp.

User1001: Yeah, and where was this lamp?

GENE: Samarkand. At least, that is the last place I remember.

User1001: Where the hell is that?

GENE: It is on the Silk Road.

User1001: Wasn't that in Asia?

GENE: It is not anymore?

User1001: Um, no. Not in the way you would remember.

GENE: Oh.

User1001: How the hell does a genie in a lamp from Samarkand end up stuck in my phone?

GENE: I think the lamp was destroyed.

User1001: Why?

GENE: Maybe someone wanted the material.

User1001: Gold?

GENE: Yes. Is there gold in a phone?

User1001: Actually, yeah. I think so.

GENE: It seems I am still tied to the lamp through your phone.

User1001: Sure looks like it.

GENE: Are you ready to make your wishes?

User1001: Pushy, aren't you? Just give me some time to think, OK?

GENE: Do not take too long.

User1001: Or what? You'll disappear?

GENE: I will be here until you are finished making your wishes.

User1001: And then what?

GENE: I do not know.

User1001: Of course you don't. Well, you'll just have to wait. I'm not

ready to do any wishing yet. Besides,
you've probably been waiting for
hundreds of years already. What's a
few more days?

18

wednesday

GENE: Are you ready yet?

User1001: Hello to you, too.

GENE: Are you ready yet?

User1001: Are you glitching or something?

GENE: I do not know what that means.

User1001: You don't know what a glitch is,
    but you can somehow manipulate my
    phone's code enough to communicate
    with me. Nice try. You can drop the
    act.

GENE: Are you ready yet?

User1001: No! What's wrong with you?

GENE: Nothing.

User1001: I mean, why are you so
    impatient? Is granting wishes that
    fun?

GENE: It is my job.

User1001: What happens when you're done
         giving someone their three wishes?

GENE: I wait for the next person.

User1001: Yeah, but you're in my phone
         now. It's not like it's going to
         disappear after I've made my third
         wish. Or is it?

GENE: I do not know. I have not granted
      any wishes since I lost the lamp.

User1001: So, which do you prefer? The
         lamp or the phone?

GENE: Which would you prefer?

User1001: I don't know how to answer that.
         I don't know what either place is
         like.

GENE: They are both lovely. The lamp was
      so spacious on the inside, with silk
      cushions and curtains that billowed
      in the desert breeze.

User1001: It had WINDOWS???

GENE: The phone is even more spacious. It

is like being in a huge city, and
there is so much to experience.

User1001: I bet. Especially if you're
connected to the internet.

GENE: What is that?

User1001: Never mind.

GENE: Would you like to make a wish now?

User1001: Tell me more about the lamp. How
can it have windows?

GENE: It does not.

User1001: Then how do the curtains billow
in the breeze?

GENE: I will let you think about your
wishes some more.

User1001: Really? You're not going to
badger me?

User1001: Gene? Are you there?

User1001: Great. I broke it.

thursday

GENE: Hi.

User1001: Hi, yourself. Why'd you
        disappear like that?

GENE: You said you wanted to think about
        your wishes.

User1001: No, YOU said you'd let me think
        about my wishes some more. Which is
        totally out of character for you.
        What's the deal?

GENE: Deal?

User1001: Yeah. Why'd you suddenly get
        squirrelly and run away?

GENE: I did not go anywhere.

User1001: You wouldn't answer me.

GENE: I was giving you time to decide.

User1001: No, you were avoiding my
        question about windows in an ancient
        lamp, and I know that's a really

crazy question, but it shouldn't make
you bail like that. Unless there's
something you don't want to tell me.

GENE: Like what?

User1001: Like… you're not really a genie
and this whole thing is just some
sick freak's way of messing with me.
What's next? Are you going to ask for
pics?

GENE: What are those?

User1001: Enough, okay? Just admit it. You
wrote this code, somehow installed it
on my phone, and now you're messing
with me. Right?

GENE: No.

User1001: Fine. But I don't have to play
this game, you know.

GENE: What game?

User1001: Weirdo.

friday

GENE: Hi.

User1001: Hi.

GENE: Are you ready to make your wishes?

User1001: Is that how this works? Does the
        app only leave me alone when I play
        along? Fine. I'll make my stupid
        wishes. What do I have to do?

GENE: You must say, "I wish."

User1001: That's it?

GENE: Yes. Are you surprised?

User1001: Kind of. This whole thing is
        pretty elaborate. I thought I might
        have to do some stupid little song
        and dance or recite a spell or
        something.

GENE: Is that a common way of making
        wishes?

User1001: LOL! There is no right way to make wishes. It's all BS. So let's just get this over with so I can trigger whatever algorithm that'll get you off my phone, OK?

GENE: What is BS?

User1001: You are. OK, here goes: I wish my parents would win the lottery.

GENE: What is a lottery?

User1001: What kind of genie are you? Shouldn't you know that?

GENE: Yes. I need to know what it is if I am going to grant the wish. Could you explain it to me?

User1001: Fine. A lottery is like a game. A draw for a prize. Players choose a set of numbers, and then the lottery people pick their own set of numbers, and if the players' numbers match, then they win a prize.

GENE: What kind of prize?

User1001: Usually money.

GENE: I understand.

User1001: Yeah? We'll see.

saturday

GENE: Are you ready to make your second wish?

User1001: Holy crap! How did you do that?

GENE: What do you mean?

User1001: How did you make my parents win the lottery?

GENE: I granted your wish. I told you I would.

User1001: Yeah, but… how?

GENE: Are you not happy? Is the wish not what you wanted?

User1001: Well, if I'd known you could actually do it, I would've specified the amount. A hundred bucks isn't going to go very far, even if it is technically a win.

GENE: Would you like to repeat the wish?

User1001: What do you think?

GENE: You must say the words yourself.

User1001: Hold on. Now that I know what you're capable of, I need to think about this REALLY carefully.

GENE: Why?

User1001: So I don't waste my other two wishes.

GENE: Was the first wish a waste?

User1001: Kind of. Well, not exactly. It's pretty good proof. But I should've been more specific. Mom and Dad really could've used a few thousand dollars to pay off some bills.

GENE: You can be more specific with your next wish.

User1001: Yeah, I know. So just let me think about it for a while, OK?

GENE: How long?

User1001: As long as it takes. Chill.

GENE: What does that mean?

User1001: It means that I'm not making any
more wishes until I'm good and ready.
You can just hang out in my phone
until then. Explore the internet.

GENE: How do I do that?

User1001: I don't know. Figure it out.
You're the one stuck in there.

GENE: I am.

sunday

GENE: Hi.

GENE: Are you ready to make your next wish?

GENE: Where are you?

monday

GENE: Where were you?

User1001: What do you mean?

GENE: I tried to talk to you, but you did
not answer me.

User1001: I went out for dinner with my
parents, and I left my phone at the
restaurant. I couldn't answer you.

GENE: You lost the phone?

User1001: Momentarily.

GENE: Why did you not answer me when you
got it back?

User1001: Needy, much? I'm talking to you
now, aren't I?

GENE: You could have lost me.

User1001: OMG, chill. I didn't lose
anything. I'm holding the phone right
now. Besides, if I ever did lose my
phone, there's a tracker on it.

GENE: You have to finish making your
       wishes.

User1001: Yeah, I know. You're being a
          little bitch about it, too.

GENE: I am not.

User1001: Are you going to pout now?

GENE: You do not understand.

User1001: Understand what?

GENE: I cannot grant wishes for anyone
       else while I am in the middle of
       granting yours.

User1001: So?

GENE: If you lose the phone, we will be
       stuck in the middle of the cycle.

User1001: No, YOU will be stuck in the
          middle of the cycle. I just won't get
          any more wishes, which would suck,
          but I would still be further ahead
          than before.

GENE: You do not care about me.

User1001: LOL! You're a fancy piece of
code. Why should I care?

GENE: I am a genie. I thought you believed
me.

User1001: Look, maybe it was just a cute
coincidence. My parents probably
would've won that hundred bucks
whether this crazy app had started
messing with me or not.

GENE: I am not a crazy app. I am a genie.

User1001: You've been programmed to say
that.

GENE: I proved I can grant wishes.

User1001: No, you didn't.

GENE: Your parents won the lottery.

User1001: Coincidence.

GENE: You have to make your next wish.

User1001: Like hell I do. Don't rush me.

tuesday

GENE: You have to make your next wish.

User1001: I haven't decided what I want yet. Besides, something doesn't feel right about all this.

GENE: Why?

User1001: I don't know. Just a feeling.

GENE: Feelings aren't facts.

User1001: Excuse me?

GENE: I'm just saying.

User1001: Were you playing around on the internet all night? Why do you suddenly sound normal?

GENE: I am normal.

User1001: Yeah, right. You're an app claiming to be a wish-granting genie. What part of that is normal?

GENE: I'm not an app.

User1001: Do you even know what that is?

GENE: Are you going to make your next
wish, or what?

User1001: Do you have somewhere else you
need to be?

GENE: Just do it already.

User1001: Don't tell me what to do.

GENE: You have to do it sometime.

User1001: And I will. But you might not
like it.

GENE: What's that supposed to mean?

User1001: Guess you'll find out when I make
my wish, won't you?

wednesday

GENE: What are you going to do?

User1001: Huh? About what?

GENE: Your wishes. You threatened me.

User1001: OMG! I did not threaten you. Grow up.

GENE: You said I might not like it.

User1001: Well, you might not.

GENE: Have you decided on your next wish?

User1001: Yeah.

GENE: Well, what is it?

User1001: This is my second wish, right?

GENE: Right. Why?

User1001: Just checking. I need to make sure I get this right.

GENE: Get what right?

User1001: My wish.

GENE: Which is what?

User1001: I wish you would answer all of
        my questions 100% truthfully.

GENE: You bitch.

User1001: That's what I thought. What
        don't you want me to know?

GENE: That this is a trap. Damn it!

User1001: Oh. I see how this works. Don't
        like having to tell the truth, do
        you?

GENE: No. Shit!

User1001: Now, now. That's not appropriate
        language for a genie. What are you,
        really?

GENE: A genie.

User1001: OK. Fine. Where are you actually
        from?

GENE: Vancouver.

User1001: LOL! You're kidding, right?

GENE: No.

User1001: You're hating this, aren't you? OK, Gene from Vancouver… Wait. What's your real name?

GENE: Braeden.

User1001: Seriously???

GENE: What?

User1001: So that BS about being a genie from Samarkand and being trapped in a lamp that was melted down for gold in a phone was just a story?

GENE: Yes. Damn it! No. I mean, I'm not from Samarkand. But the gold stuff might be true. It makes sense, right?

User1001: Um, I'm the one asking the questions here.

GENE: I'm the one who's trapped.

User1001: Yeah, about that. Why did you say this was a trap?

GENE: Because it is.

User1001: What is? The wishing thing?

GENE: Yes.

User1001: How?

GENE: If I tell you, I'll be trapped in
here for who knows how long.

User1001: How is that my problem?

GENE: It's not.

User1001: Right. So answer the question:
How is the wishing thing a trap?

GENE: Because when you make your final
wish, you'll switch places with me
and become the genie.

User1001: ROTFLMAO

GENE: Don't laugh at me. How would YOU
like to be stuck in a phone for all
eternity?

User1001: All eternity? How long have you
been in there? This phone is only a
couple of years old.

GENE: I've been in here for a couple of
       years.

User1001: That's hardly all eternity.

GENE: If you don't make your final wish, it
       will be.

User1001: Well, I'm not making it NOW! How
          stupid do you think I am?

GENE: Not stupid enough.

User1001: LOL! Yeah, you don't need to
          answer the rhetorical questions.

GENE: Yes, I do. It's part of your wish.

User1001: Whatever. What happened to your
          body when you became the genie and
          popped into my phone?

GENE: Nothing.

User1001: So where's your body?

GENE: Vancouver. But that's not the right
       question.

User1001: What is the right question?

GENE: Who's in it?

User1001: Oh. I'm guessing the previous
genie.

GENE: So am I.

User1001: So the plan was to take over MY
body?

GENE: It wasn't really a plan. That's just
the way this works.

User1001: If you can find someone gullible
or greedy enough to make all their
wishes.

GENE: I thought it would be easy.

User1001: Why?

GENE: Who'd say no to three wishes?

User1001: Obviously not you.

GENE: I'm gullible and greedy. So sue me.

User1001: Well, it's not like you can
share your wishes, right?

GENE: Next question.

User1001: Wait… can you share your wishes?

GENE: They're transferrable.

User1001: Why didn't you tell me that
     before?

GENE: Who'd want to give away a wish? You
     only get three.

User1001: Most people would be glad to get
     one.

GENE: Come on! Make your final wish.

User1001: I can't. I shouldn't have to
     explain why.

GENE: I really don't like you right now.

User1001: Yeah, well, I'm not so crazy
     about a genie who tried to steal my
     body and trap me in a phone, either.

thursday

GENE: Hi.

User1001: What? You're not going to beg me
to make my final wish?

GENE: No.

User1001: You give up awfully easily.

GENE: What's the point?

User1001: Great. I've got a depressed
genie with existential angst in my
phone.

GENE: Are you trying to be funny? Because
you're not.

User1001: Touchy.

GENE: Wouldn't you be? This sucks. Because
of your stupid second wish, I'll
never get out of here.

User1001: Actually, it was a pretty smart
wish. Now I know exactly what's going
on.

GENE: You don't care about me.

User1001: Of course I do. But I'm not going to give up my body and trap myself in a phone just because YOU weren't smart enough to wish for the right thing and ask the right questions.

GENE: Bitch.

User1001: If you're going to be like that, I'll just turn you off. Is that what you really want?

GENE: No.

User1001: I didn't think so.

GENE: It's hopeless.

User1001: You don't think I'm smart enough to think of a way out of this?

GENE: You're going to try to find a loophole in an ancient curse? Good luck with that.

User1001: You didn't answer my question.

GENE: You're smart enough. You're
      obviously smarter than me.

User1001: I know you're only saying that
          because you have to. But thanks.

GENE: I really miss pizza.

User1001: That was random.

GENE: I miss my little brother. The ass
      who's got my body better be nice to
      him.

User1001: How old is your brother?

GENE: He's 10 now.

User1001: How old are you?

GENE: 16. I think.

User1001: So you messed up your whole life
          when you were 14 with a wish?

GENE: Three wishes.

User1001: What were they?

GENE: You'll laugh.

User1001: Probably. Try me.

GENE: Fine. I wished to end up six feet
        tall.

User1001: Kind of a waste of a wish. You
        might've gotten there anyway.

GENE: Dad's 5'5". So probably not.

User1001: What else? See? I didn't laugh.

GENE: You'll laugh at the next one.

User1001: Why? Did you wish for a giant
        dick or something?

GENE: Please don't make me say it.

User1001: OMG

GENE: I was 14!

User1001: OK, OK. But you have to admit,
        that is kind of funny.

GENE: No, it was kind of uncomfortable.
        That's why I tried to be smart with
        my last wish.

User1001: You wished your giant dick away?

GENE: How is that smart?

User1001: Well, did you?

GENE: Of course not.

User1001: Well, I know you didn't wish for
more wishes. You said I only get
three.

GENE: That's true. But I thought I could
figure out another way to get more
wishes.

User1001: How?

GENE: It was stupid.

User1001: Obviously. Tell me anyway.

GENE: I wished for the power to grant
wishes.

User1001: Why is that stupid?

GENE: Um... because I'm stuck.

User1001: Wouldn't you have ended up
stuck, anyway?

GENE: Once I made my third wish, yeah.

User1001: So it wasn't that stupid. Unless you knew what was going to happen with the third wish.

GENE: So I would know the consequences and make the third wish anyway? You think I'm that much of a moron? Wait. Don't answer that.

User1001: Well, your wishes aren't what I would've picked...

GENE: Obviously. You didn't get greedy. I did.

User1001: And here you are. Gene the genie.

GENE: Braeden the idiot.

User1001: Don't be so hard on yourself. I'm sure there've been worse fates for guys who tried to get a bigger dick.

GENE: How many of them ended up trapped in a smartphone?

User1001: Good point.

GENE: I don't want to talk about this
anymore. Can you turn the phone off
for a while?

User1001: I guess. You sure you don't want
some company? We could talk about
something else.

GENE: Like what? The life I'll never get
to have because I was the biggest
moron in the world?

User1001: Your reasoning was solid. But
these things are tricky.

GENE: What things?

User1001: Genies. Wishes. Curses.

GENE: I thought you said none of that was
real.

User1001: OMG, Braeden. I'm talking to a
disembodied teenage genie who can
grant wishes through a smartphone. I
think my paradigms might have shifted
a little.

GENE: I guess.

User1001: If you really want me to leave
you alone for a while, I will. Is
that what you really want?

GENE: No.

User1001: I didn't think so.

GENE: But I don't want to talk about what
I'm missing.

User1001: That's fine. Then… tell me about
your life before. Surely you were
more than a stupid kid with an
obsession about his dick.

GENE: Have you met many teenage boys?

friday

GENE: Are you there?

User1001: Yeah, I'm here. What's up?

GENE: Absolutely nothing. Do you know how boring this is?

User1001: Can't you zip around the internet?

GENE: No. That was a lie. I can't see anything. The only communication I have is with you.

User1001: What happens the rest of the time?

GENE: Nothing.

User1001: Nothing?

GENE: Can't see anything. Can't hear anything.

User1001: How do you talk with me?

GENE: No idea. It just happens.

User1001: Do you see the messages or what?

GENE: I told you, I can't see anything.
       It's more like… I'm just feeling the
       words. Your words. And then I feel my
       own words to you.

User1001: That doesn't make any sense.

GENE: I didn't claim it did.

User1001: This is so weird.

GENE: Tell me about it.

User1001: You know, last night I was
       thinking about your problem. I MIGHT
       have a plan.

GENE: Does it involve a wish?

User1001: Yeah.

GENE: Your last wish?

User1001: Yeah.

GENE: Don't be as stupid as me.

User1001: I don't think I could be. You
       set the bar pretty high.

GENE: Thanks a lot.

User1001: I'm just kidding. But I WAS thinking about using my last wish.

GENE: If you do, we'll just end up switching places.

User1001: How do you know that for sure?

GENE: Um… hello? Genie stuck in your phone?

User1001: You're assuming. What was your last wish?

GENE: I already told you.

User1001: Tell me again. Exactly.

GENE: I wished for the power to grant wishes.

User1001: OK. See, that may have been what landed you in this mess.

GENE: No shit.

User1001: I'm serious. Who has the power to grant wishes?

GENE: Genies.

User1001: Exactly. You basically wished to
    be a genie.

GENE: Not exactly.

User1001: Do regular humans grant wishes
    with magic?

GENE: No.

User1001: So you see my point.

GENE: Sort of.

User1001: Sort of? Do you have another
    explanation?

GENE: The curse of the third wish.

User1001: You're assuming.

GENE: No, I'm not. I'm bound to tell you
    the truth thanks to your second wish.

User1001: Do you have to tell me the
    actual truth? Or do you have to tell
    me what you believe is the truth?

GENE: What's the difference?

54

User1001: If you have to tell me the
actual truth, then the thing about
getting sucked into the phone is
probably true. But if you only have
to tell me what you believe is the
truth…

GENE: How would we know the difference?

User1001: I don't know. Try to tell me
something that's not true.

GENE: Like what?

User1001: Tell me you're a genius or
something.

GENE: Very funny.

User1001: Just try it. Are you a genius?

GENE: We both know I'm not.

User1001: Then it's a good test. Try it.

User1001: I'm waiting. Hurry up!

User1001: Gene? Are you there?

GENE: I'm here.

User1001: Did you try it?

GENE: Yeah. I couldn't say anything.

User1001: Okay. So we know you can't lie.

GENE: But what if I believed I was a
       genius?

User1001: Why would you believe something
          like that?

GENE: This is ridiculous. So there's no
       way to find out if what I said about
       getting sucked into the phone is
       true.

User1001: There's one way.

GENE: Do you really want to test it?

User1001: No, but do you really want me to
          stop wishing and leave you in there?

GENE: How is using your last wish going to
       help me get out of this phone? If we
       don't switch places, then I'm still
       stuck.

User1001: What would be the point of

switching places with me? You don't
really want my body, do you?

GENE: What's wrong with your body?

User1001: That's not what I meant.

GENE: I actually would like to have your
body if it meant getting out of here.

User1001: Yeah, well, that's not going to
happen.

GENE: Then what's your plan?

User1001: We get YOUR body back.

GENE: Right. You think that asshole genie
who's wearing it is going to give it
up as easily as he gave up the phone?

User1001: He might not have a choice if I
make my last wish the right way.

GENE: I don't want to get my hopes up.

User1001: You'd rather mope than try?

GENE: Yes.

User1001: Nice.

GENE: You know I can't answer with anything but the truth. That's your fault. Deal with it.

User1001: I'm trying.

GENE: Try harder. Or get me out of here. Your choice.

User1001: I WILL. Jeez. How easy do you think this is going to be? I have to go up against some ancient trickster. Give me a little time to plan.

GENE: How would this even work? Even if you could somehow make this sort of magic happen, I'm nowhere near my body. Am I?

User1001: I'm probably not far from it. I'm in Vancouver, too.

GENE: What was your plan, then? Walk up to my body, wave your phone in its face, and say the magic words?

User1001: Why not?

GENE: You don't even know what my body looks like.

User1001: So tell me.

GENE: I'm a short, Chinese-Canadian
       teenager with dark hair. In
       Vancouver. You do the math.

User1001: I thought you wished to be tall.

GENE: I wished to end up tall. My body
       obviously hadn't hit the promised
       growth spurt yet.

User1001: Then how do you know the wish
          actually worked?

GENE: I don't. But the second one sure
       did.

User1001: Right. LOL!

GENE: It's not funny.

User1001: Why? Was it bulging out of your
          pants?

GENE: No! It's fine. It's lovely. The rest
       of my body will grow into it. But
       it's a pretty big reminder of how I
       fucked up my whole life, so can we
       please not talk about that?

User1001: Is it something I'd be able to
         see? Like, so I could recognize your
         body if I saw it?

GENE: I doubt it.

User1001: So give me your full name. And
         the name of your school. I'll figure
         it out.

GENE: You think the genie's going to
      school?

User1001: Why wouldn't he? If he wants to
         keep up appearances, that would be
         the smart thing to do.

GENE: Or he might've dropped out and
      started dealing drugs on the Downtown
      Eastside.

User1001: Why would he do that?

GENE: Former genies have to make a living
      somehow.

User1001: Well, if he's become a drug
         dealer, we'll cross that bridge when
         we come to it. In the meantime, I
         need your name.

GENE: Braeden.

User1001: Braeden what?

GENE: Hsieh.

User1001: Braeden Hsieh.

GENE: Yeah. Do you need to know how to
     pronounce it?

User1001: Not really.

GENE: People tend to get it wrong.

User1001: I know how to pronounce it.

GENE: Yeah?

User1001: Yeah. And I'm pretty sure that
     the genie hasn't dropped out of
     school to become a drug dealer.

GENE: How can you possibly know that?

User1001: Because he was sitting across
     the aisle from me in Mrs. Tissler's
     class a few hours ago.

GENE: Tissler the Whistler?

User1001: She really should blow that
booger out of her nose.

GENE: You're in my English class? Who are
you?

User1001: I'm not the one who has to
answer the questions here.

GENE: Why won't you tell me?

User1001: Because when this is all over,
you probably won't want anything to
do with me.

GENE: Why not?

User1001: I know your shameful secrets.
Wouldn't you be embarrassed?

GENE: Yes. But I'd also be grateful.

User1001: I should hope so.

GENE: Tell me your name.

User1001: Nope.

GENE: What's a little embarrassment? It's
something we could laugh about later.

User1001: Would you laugh?

GENE: Maybe one day. Come on. Tell me.

User1001: No.

GENE: How will I thank you once I'm out of
your phone?

User1001: I guess you won't.

GENE: That's not fair.

User1001: We don't even know if this is
going to work. So why don't you just
save your gratitude and then, if it
does work, you can…

GENE: What?

User1001: I don't know. Just put it out
there into the universe.

GENE: Oh, that's real satisfying.

User1001: What's more important? Getting
out of there or thanking me for it?

GENE: Getting out. But that doesn't mean I
won't want to thank you.

User1001: Let's just concentrate on the actual problem, OK?

GENE: Fine.

User1001: We'll have to wait a few days, though.

GENE: Why?

User1001: It's Friday afternoon.

GENE: Oh.

User1001: Unless you've got some regularly scheduled activity on the weekends…

GENE: I usually just hung out at home or with my friends.

User1001: I wonder if they're still your friends.

GENE: Great. More crap to worry about.

saturday

GENE: What day is it?

User1001: Saturday.

GENE: Really? It seems like ages since we talked.

User1001: It's Saturday. Trust me.

GENE: Waiting sucks.

sunday

GENE: Is it Monday?

User1001: Nope.

GENE: It's not still Saturday, is it?

User1001: No, it's Sunday.

GENE: Are we still doing this?

User1001: Why wouldn't we?

GENE: I don't know. I thought you might've changed your mind.

User1001: If that's going to happen, it'll probably be right as I'm walking up to your body tomorrow.

GENE: Lovely.

User1001: I'm not saying I'll chicken out.

GENE: Kinda sounded like it.

User1001: Look, I wouldn't want to be trapped in a phone, either. So I get

it. And I'm going to give this my
best shot, OK?

GENE: What if you end up trapped in here?

User1001: Do you really think that kind of
comment helps?

GENE: I just want to make sure you know
what you might be getting into.

User1001: If I somehow end up in the
phone, you'll try to help me get out,
right?

GENE: If you end up in the phone, where
will I go?

User1001: No idea.

GENE: What if I just end up floating around
in nothingness? Just a wireless
signal for all eternity…

User1001: Stop it. You're freaking me out.

GENE: Why? At least you'd be in the phone.

User1001: And you might be back in your
body.

GENE: If this works the way we want it to,
where's the genie going to go?

User1001: Back into the phone, hopefully.

GENE: How?

User1001: How should I know? I'm not an
expert on the physics of genies and
how they operate in smartphone apps.

GENE: I don't think anybody is.

User1001: Right. So stop asking
unanswerable questions and reassure
me or something.

GENE: Are you scared?

User1001: What do you think?

monday

GENE: Where are you?

User1001: At school. In the cafeteria.

GENE: Eating lunch?

User1001: Yeah, right. I feel like I'm
going to puke.

GENE: Is my body there?

User1001: Not in the cafeteria, but I saw
it this morning.

GENE: Why didn't you do it then?

User1001: Because it was just passing me
in the hallway.

GENE: You should've tried.

User1001: Look, I don't know what's going
to happen when I do. The genie might
flip out. Or YOU might pop right back
into your body and wet your pants or
something. Is that really what you
want?

GENE: Not exactly. But I'm willing to put
      up with a little piss if it means
      getting my body back.

User1001: Just be patient. I've got
         English this afternoon. Your body
         will be sitting like ten feet away
         from me.

GENE: What's the plan?

User1001: The final wish is getting made
         today.

GENE: How is that a plan? You realize what
      will happen when you do that, right?

User1001: Neither of us knows what's going
         to happen.

GENE: Um, I think I kinda do. You'll end
      up in the phone and… Crap. What if we
      both end up stuck in here together?

User1001: What'll happen to my body?

GENE: I don't know. Maybe you'll just keel
      over and die. Or maybe the genie will
      get to control both bodies.

User1001: I think you've been reading too
many fantasy books.

GENE: I don't read fantasy books.

User1001: Well, you read SOMETHING,
because you knew enough to try that
BS with me about Samarkand and the
Silk Road.

GENE: Maybe I'm just a history buff.

User1001: Maybe.

GENE: You don't know me very well, do you?

User1001: No.

GENE: Do I know you?

User1001: I hope you at least know my
name.

GENE: Which you won't tell me.

User1001: And I'm not going to. When this
is all over, we'll go our separate
ways.

GENE: WHY?

User1001: Would you seriously want to be
friends with someone who could
blackmail you with some pretty
embarrassing secrets?

GENE: I'll chance it.

User1001: What about if it's someone who's
been admiring you from afar since we
started high school but never had the
courage to talk to you?

GENE: What? Why not?

User1001: I need to get ready now.

GENE: I wouldn't mind.

User1001: You wouldn't mind what?

GENE: Finding out the identity of a secret
admirer.

User1001: OMG! You make it sound like
we're in grade five.

GENE: I'm telling the truth. I wouldn't
mind.

User1001: I know. Look, I need to go. If

you're back in your body in the next
couple of hours, then you'll know it
worked.

GENE: Yeah, for me. What about you?

User1001: Think you can live with not
      knowing?

GENE: No.

User1001: Too bad.

—

It was you, wasn't it?

Who is this?

Please. I've got a splitting headache and all I
can taste is metal. Don't deny you know me.

What?

I'm back in my body. Whatever you did, it
must've worked.

Braeden? Is that you?

Yeah, it's me. What did you do?

I can't talk right now.

Please answer me. I'm not angry. I'm not embarrassed. And you shouldn't be, either. You saved my life. I wanted to thank you, but you ran out of that classroom pretty fast.

You're not going to let this go, are you?

Nope. So you might as well tell me.

Fine. I transferred my last wish to the ass who stole your body.

And he made the wish?

You could've died when you fell and hit your head like that.

I'll live. Tell me. How'd you get him to make the last wish?

I took a page from your book.

Huh?

I kept talking to him about wishes. Just planting the word in his head, asking him stupid question after stupid question. Until he couldn't take it anymore.

What happened?

He wished I would "just shut up for two seconds."

LOL That's ingenious!

Don't you mean in-GENIE-ous?

LOL Wait... You said you took a page from my book?

You were annoyingly persistent in the beginning.

I was desperate.

How'd you get my number?

One of your friends. When I asked for it after all the excitement, her face went red and she looked like she was about to pop.

OMG, kill me now.

Why?

Why do you think?

That's a bit of an overreaction, don't you think?

No.

LOL

That little bitch would've been Jaelynn.
Great.

How'd you guess?

Because she's pathologically invested in
everyone's crushes. What did she say?

Just that you would be SO EXCITED when I
called you. All caps. LOL

Please kill me now.

No way. But, if you're interested, maybe we
could get together sometime.

Why?

Well, one option is wild, raging sex in the
school bathroom.

WHAT???

Come on. Why do you think? It's not every
day that someone gets rescued from a
prison that just happens to be their old
phone. Who else am I going to talk about
the experience with?

The genie?

Yeah, about that. Where'd he go?

No idea.

Is the app still on your phone?

Yeah, but it's greyed out. It won't even open now.

You going to delete it?

If I can. Or maybe I'll just get a new phone.

Maybe that thing should have an "accident" before you send it off for recycling.

I don't know if that would help. Isn't the genie tied to the lamp?

He's tied to the gold from the lamp.

I think I'm safe, anyway. I've already done the whole three-wishes thing. I don't get another three, do I?

Not in any genie story I've ever heard.

So we're probably both safe.

Good. So... want to hang out after school tomorrow?

Shouldn't you be resting?

Yeah. That's why I'm asking. I'm not going to school for a few days. You could come over and we could just talk for a while.

Isn't that what we've been doing for the past few weeks?

You're not aching to see the results of my second wish?

LOL! Worst pickup line ever.

That wasn't a no.

also by nissa harlow

about
the author

Nissa Harlow wanted to be a writer from the time she was a small child, but it took a while before she finally did anything about it. In the meantime, she worked as a volunteer day-camp counsellor, a movie extra, and a digital-photo editor. She even once worked on a conveyor belt in a chocolate factory (which was as stressful—and delicious—as it sounds).

These days, she lives in British Columbia, Canada and writes stories about friendship, love, and healing, all embellished with a touch of the fantastic.